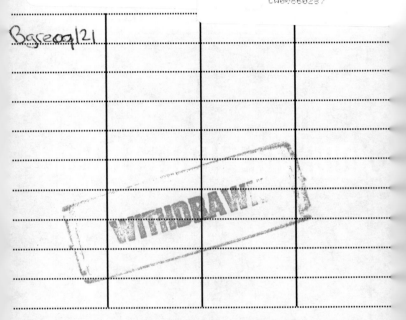

Raintree is an imprint of Capstone Global Library Limited, a company
incorporated in England and Wales having its registered office at 264
Banbury Road, Oxford, OX2 7DY – Registered company number: 6695582

www.raintree.co.uk
myorders@raintree.co.uk

Designed by Hilary Wacholz
Original illustrations © Capstone Global Library Limited 2022
Originated by Capstone Global Library Ltd
Printed and bound in India

978 1 3982 1360 9

British Library Cataloguing in Publication Data
A full catalogue record for this book is available from the British Library.

CONTENTS

The Library of Doom is a hidden fortress.
It holds the world's largest collection
of strange and dangerous books.

Behold the Librarian. He defends the Library – and
the world – from super-villains, clever thieves
and fierce monsters. Many of his adventures
have remained secret. Now they can be told.

SECRET #75
ALL BOOKS HAVE ENDINGS, BUT
SOME STORIES ARE ENDLESS.

Chapter One

MOTHER GHOUL'S

Young Harry Hubbard sits on a train. He sits at the very back with a STRANGE book on his lap.

Harry found the book in his grandmother's ATTIC.

He posted about the book online. A guy called <u>Jack</u> said he wanted to buy it.

Now Harry is on his way to meet Jack.

The train enters a long, **DARK** tunnel.

In the dark, the book's title glows.

Harry flicks through the book. The titles of the **WEIRD** nursery rhymes glow.

JACK AND JILL
TUMBLE FOREVER

HUMPTY DUMPTY'S
ENDLESS DIVE

LONDON BRIDGE IS
ALWAYS FALLING

Harry **SHIVERS**. The pictures on the pages frighten him.

Chapter Two

FALLING DOWN, FALLING DOWN

WHUMP!

The train hits a bump, and the book
FALLS onto the floor.

The book drops into the aisle.

The book is **KNOCKED** open.

WHUMP!

Another bump knocks Harry from his seat. He falls towards the open book.

Harry's **HEAD** falls into the book.

Then his shoulders fall.

His **ENTIRE** body slips into the open book.

The train *RUSHES* out of the tunnel.

The whistle blows.

HOOOOOO-HOOOOOOOO!

None of the other passengers see what happens to Harry.

At the front of the train carriage, a small girl stands up.

She **RUNS** down the aisle towards the toilets.

The girl doesn't notice the book on the floor. She trips.

AAAAHHHHHHHH-HHHHHHHHH!!

The girl **SCREAMS** as she falls into the book.

The little girl's mother stands up at the sound. She looks around.

But she can't see her daughter ANYWHERE.

Chapter Three

ALL THE PEOPLE

The girl is still screaming. She is falling through a **DARK**, empty space.

She sees a boy falling far below her. Then she hears a **SHOUT!**

The girl looks up and sees a man falling towards her.

"What is happening?" the man **SCREAMS**. "Where did the train go?"

A **STRANGE** woman appears from the darkness. She is falling next to the girl.

She wears old-fashioned clothes and holds a bucket of water.

The woman smiles. "Have you seen my brother, Jack?" she asks. "I've been falling for the **LONGEST** time."

The girl looks around. Now she sees **MORE** people falling.

Some fall quickly. Some fall slowly. There are even a few animals.

A cow **TUMBLES** past her. Then comes a little dog, then some plates.

An entire flock of sheep **RUSHES** past the girl.

They all seem to be falling forever through the book.

Chapter Four

JACK

On the train, the book still sits on the floor. The cover slowly **CLOSES**.

Soon, the train stops, and all the passengers exit.

No one else falls into the **STRANGE** book.

Outside are new passengers waiting to get on the train.

One of them is a man wearing a jacket and a hat. He looks around **NERVOUSLY**.

The man in the hat **JUMPS** to the front of the queue. He wants to be first on the train.

The man **RUSHES** inside.

"Harry! Harry!" he calls.

He walks to the back of the train and calls again. But Harry is **GONE**.

Then the man sees the OLD book lying on the floor.

"There it is!" he says. "Finally."

More passengers get on the train.

The man in the hat picks up the book. He holds it TIGHTLY to his chest.

He doesn't want anyone else to **SEE** the book.

"Jack!"

The man in the hat **HEARS** someone call his name.

At the back of the train carriage stands a **TALL** figure in the shadows.

Chapter Five

UPSIDE-DOWN

"The Librarian?" whispers the man in the hat.

The figure in the **SHADOWS** steps forward.

"Yes, Jack," says the Librarian. "Now hand me the book. It escaped from my Library. It is dangerous."

Jack **SHAKES** his head. "I need this book to get my sister back."

"I promise I will **SAVE** her," says the Librarian. "But first you must give me the book."

Jack looks down at the cover. Then he slowly hands the book to the Librarian.

The hero **OPENS** it.

"Ah, this is why it's so dangerous," the Librarian says. "Someone ripped out the last page. This book is missing *THE END*."

The book is endless.

The Librarian **WAVES** his hand.

He and Jack are no longer standing in the train.

They are standing in a **DARK** meadow. The moon peeks over the top of a hill.

The Librarian opens the book and holds it **UPSIDE** down.

"*SEMYHR YRESRUN!*" he chants. "The bottom shall become the top!"

He puts the book facedown in
the **TALL** grass.

Suddenly a hand sticks out from
under the cover.

A head appears next. Soon, people and animals are **CLIMBING** out of the book.

The crowd gets larger and larger.

The little girl from the train is there. So is Harry Hubbard.

The Librarian **WAVES** his hand again.

"Back to your own stories," says the hero.

Everyone disappears – almost everyone.

One **WOMAN** remains. A bucket sits in the grass by her side.

"Jack!" cries the woman, *RUNNING* over.

"Jill!" **SHOUTS** the man in the hat.
"I thought I would never see you again."

The two hug. Then together they grab
the bucket's handle and *RUN* up the hill.

"A happy ending," the Librarian says
to himself.

He picks up the book, which is **WET** with dew.

Then the hero and the **STRANGE** book fade away into the moonlight.

GLOSSARY

aisle walkway between rows of seats on a bus or a train

chant speak with a strong rhythm

dangerous able or likely to cause harm

exit leave a place

figure shape or outline of something, especially a human

ghoul someone who enjoys doing terrible things

meadow land covered in tall grass

nursery rhyme short poem for children that often tells a story; *Mother Goose's Nursery Rhymes* has some of the most famous, with poems such as "Jack and Jill", "Mary Had a Little Lamb" and "Humpty Dumpty"

passenger person who is travelling on a train, car, bus or other vehicle

TALK ABOUT IT

1. *Mother Ghoul's Nursery Rhymes* is a dangerous book. Look back through the story and find three hints it's not normal.

2. The Librarian brought the bottomless book to an end. Were you surprised by what happened? Did you like the ending of this story? Explain your answer.

WRITE ABOUT IT

1. At first Jack didn't want to give the Librarian the book of nursery rhymes. Write a letter to Jack arguing why he should trust the Librarian and get his help.

2. This story uses the characters from the nursery rhyme "Jack and Jill". Think of another nursery rhyme. Take the characters from it and write a new, exciting story.

ABOUT THE AUTHOR

Michael Dahl is an award-winning author of more than 200 books for young people. He especially likes to write scary or weird fiction. His latest series are the sci-fi adventure Escape from Planet Alcatraz and School Bus of Horrors. As a child, Michael spent lots of time in libraries. "The creepier, the better," he says. These days, besides writing, he likes travelling and hunting for the one, true door that leads to the Library of Doom.

ABOUT THE ILLUSTRATOR

Patricio Clarey was born in 1978 in Argentina. He graduated in fine arts from the Martín A. Malharro School of Visual Arts, specializing in illustration and graphic design. Patricio currently lives in Barcelona, Spain, where he works as a freelance graphic designer and illustrator. He has created several comics and graphic novels, and his work has been featured in books and other publications.